MY FATHER'S ARMS ARE A BOAT

STEIN ERIK LUNDE
ØYVIND TORSETER

TRANSLATED FROM THE NORWEGIAN BY KARI DICKSON

ENCHANTED LION BOOKS
NEW YORK

My dad isn't listening to the radio.

He's sitting in the living room, where

the only sound is the crackling of the fire.

When I was there with him, I saw the tongues of fire lick his face.

I went over and put my hand on his arm, and he patted my hand.

Then I went into my room and got into bed.

That was a while ago now.
My bedroom door, which leads into
the living room and to him, is ajar.
"So that your dreams can come out to me,"
Daddy said when I left.

My window is pitch black.
I have socks on,
and a woolly sweater under my pyjamas.
I can't sleep.
It's quieter now than it's ever been.

I go back into the living room.

My dad looks at me, and I climb onto his lap.

He puts both his arms tight under my knees.

My body is curled up like a ball.

I rest my head against his shoulder.

My cheek is against Daddy's cheek, close to his breathing.
After a while he says: "Tomorrow we'll chop down the big spruce.
It will fall to the ground with a crash. That'll be fun, won't it?"
"Mmm," I say.
Daddy likes chopping down big trees. I know that.

"What about the red birds?" I ask.
"What about them?"
"Are they asleep?"
"They're asleep."
"In the tree?"

"They sleep here and there,"
Daddy says,
laughing a little.
"Have they eaten the bread?"
I ask.
"No, they'll have it
for breakfast."

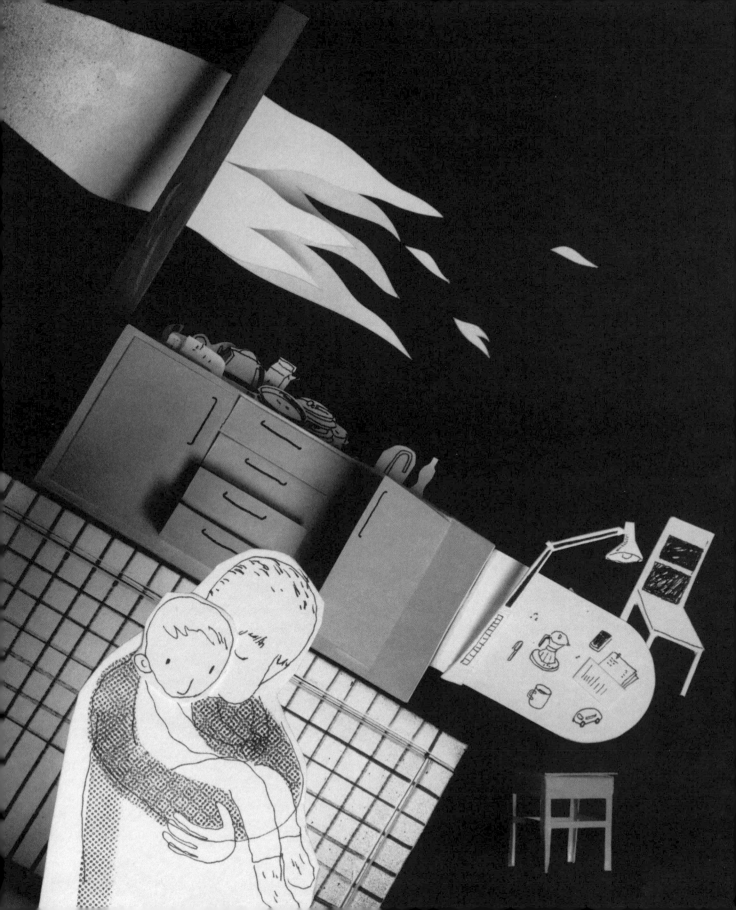

"Is the fox asleep too?" I ask.

"No, the fox is out hunting."

"What if the fox eats the birds' breakfast?"

"Then we can put out more bread."

"What if the birds wake up before us
and there's no food?"

"Everything will be all right," Daddy says.

"The fox doesn't like bread."

The red birds fly silently through the air.
They sit on the white stone and watch me with one eye.
Then they pick up pieces of bread in their beaks and
fly away to hide it somewhere high up in a tree.

Then they come back again.

They fly back and forth, until there is no bread left on the stone.

Granny says the red birds are dead people.

She told me that when we were at the old people's home.

She can hardly talk,

but I knew what she meant.

Daddy laughed when she said that.

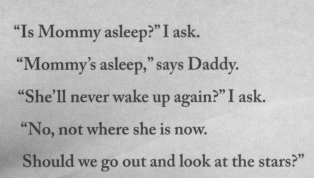

"Is Mommy asleep?" I ask.

"Mommy's asleep," says Daddy.

"She'll never wake up again?" I ask.

"No, not where she is now.

Should we go out and look at the stars?"

Daddy gets his sheepskin coat and puts it on the floor.

He puts me down on it and does up all the buttons.

Then he lifts me up so I'm lying on my back in his arms.

My bottom hangs down.

"Baa, baa black sheep," Daddy sings.

Then we go out.

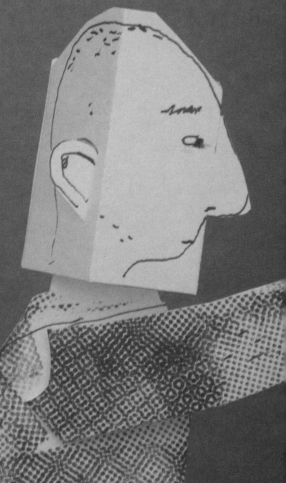

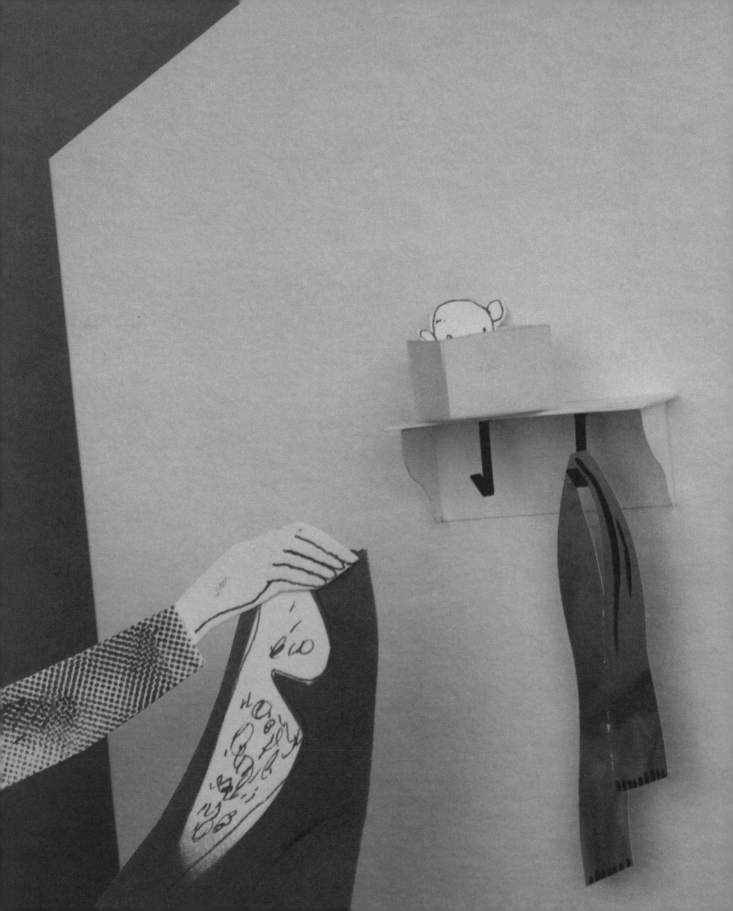

He opens the door with my dangling feet.

Out on the steps, I hear him put his clogs on below me.

Clack-clack, clack-clack down the steps.

It's cold on my face.

I look up at the stars.

I look at the moon that looks like a boat.

My dad's arms are like a boat, too.

One that sails me out into the middle of the yard.

The boat stops.

The stars are so far away and yet so close.

"If you see a shooting star, you can make a wish," Daddy says.
"I know."
"But you can't tell anyone what it is."
"I know."

There's no bread on the white stone.

We wait.

I tell myself I have to make my wish

at the very same moment

that I see the shooting star.

We wait a bit longer.

Then I see it.

Then it's gone.

I lean my head back and look up at Daddy.

His chin rubs against my forehead.

His throat swallows against my head.

I wonder if he made a wish.

I wonder if he wished the same as me.

I wonder if our wish will come true if we wished for the same thing.

Then Daddy turns me around and lifts me up.

We look straight into each other's eyes.

His eyes, black as night,

are dark and deep in his face.

When we get back inside I'm tired.

Daddy takes me out of his coat.

I tell him I'm tired.

"You can sleep on my lap," he says.

We watch the fire for a long time.

I still can't fall asleep.

"Everything will be all right," says Daddy.

"Are you sure?"

"I'm sure."

First American edition published in 2013 by
Enchanted Lion Books, 351 Van Brunt Street,
Brooklyn, NY 11231

Originally published in Norwegian as *Eg Kan Ikkje Sove No*
by Det Norske Samlaget © 2008

Text © Stein Erik Lunde
Translation © 2013, Kari Dickson

Illustration © Øyvind Torseter
Design: Elisabeth Moseng

All rights reserved in accordance with the provisions
of the Copyright Act of 1956 as amended.

A CIP record is on file with the Library of Congress
ISBN: 978-1-59270-124-7

Printed in China by South China Printing Company
Second printing, March, 2014